Tempted

Ayshia Monroe

SADDLEBACK
EDUCATIONAL PUBLISHING

2/13

PA

Bein' Good

Blind Trust

Diva

Doin' It

The Fake Date

Fitting In

Holding Back

Keepin' Her Man

Stalked

Tempted

SADDLEBACK
EDUCATIONAL PUBLISHING
www.sdlback.com

ISBN-13: 978-1-61651-670-3
ISBN-10: 1-61651-670-4
eBook: 978-1-61247-642-1

Printed in Guangzhou, China
0812/CA21201147

16 15 14 13 12   1 2 3 4 5

D amn that Jackson Beauford," Nishell Saunders muttered to herself as she walked down the hill to the river's edge. Her treasured Nikon Coolpix digital camera clomped against her white peasant blouse; she felt a bead of sweat roll down her tawny forehead.

It was so hot on this late Tuesday afternoon in June that her sandals seemed to stick to the sun-baked asphalt path. Right before Nishell had left the day-care where she was working as a summer counselor, she'd checked an outdoor thermometer. Ninety-two in the shade. Waiting for the bus that brought her here, it had felt like two hundred and ninety-two.

"Damn that Jackson," she repeated. Most days, the asphalt path along the river was filled with people walking, bicycling, rollerblading, or just tossing bread to the ducks. Not this day, though. Just too hot. "He makes me mad. Why'd I even show up?"

"Yo! Nishell! Yo! Up here!"

Nishell turned and saw Jackson standing under a weeping willow about fifty yards away. He looked better than any eleventh-grade boy should, in baggy khaki shorts and a white-ribbed undershirt beneath a paisley short-sleeve shirt. Nishell knew that his handsome face framed startling blue eyes—not so common for a brother.

Nishell thought of all the reasons she had to stay angry at Jackson. He'd flunked all his classes last semester at South Central High School. She'd told him that he could forget about hittin' it with her if he couldn't even manage D-minuses. Jackson had taken Nishell's declaration badly. He'd—

"Hey!" Jackson called. "Whatchu wanna do, Nishell? Stand there and melt into a pool of the sweetest chocolate in America? I wouldn't mind a honey dip, but I think I want you whole, you know what I'm sayin'? Come on up here, you fly girl!"

Nishell grinned.

"There's nothing finer than a man who makes you laugh," she thought. "If a man can make you laugh, you can't stay mad."

"Okay, okay." She made her way through some tall grass up to where he was standing. When she got there, she saw he'd set out a fancy picnic under the cool—well, cooler—shade of the willow.

There was even a pillow for her with a rose atop it.

"Hey. I'm glad you came," he said softly when she reached him.

She took in the picnic and cocked an eye at him. "If you worked half as hard on algebra as you did on this, you might have passed."

"Maybe," he allowed. "Course, settin' this up didn't put me to sleep like all that A-squared plus B-squared equal C-squared bull-dinky does."

"You don't have to like it," Nishell retorted. "You just have to pass it."

He raised his eyebrows. "You know how fine you look when you throw shade at me like that? Course, you look fine anyway."

Aww ...

Nishell loved it when Jackson complimented her looks. She knew she wasn't as skinny as the rest of her friends. Her clothes size started with the number "1," and she'd put herself on a diet more than once. She kept her hair long and straight and dressed to hide her major-league curves more often than not. Otherwise, every man she passed on the street made kissing noises and asked what she was hiding between them fine-lookin' twins. Today, she'd come straight from work, and she was still in jeans and the official Northeast Towers day-care yellow T-shirt.

At Jackson's invitation, she sat on the pillow. He opened a cooler and handed her a bottled iced tea, plus a plate with sliced ham, fresh potato salad, and an apple cut in half. He got the same thing for himself.

"I made all this myself," he told her.

She grabbed her camera, snapped a picture of the plate, and then took a forkful of the potato salad. It was seasoned with salt, pepper, garlic, and a little paprika. Her eyes grew wide as the tastes rolled around her tongue. "Omigod, Jackson. Where'd you learn to cook like this?"

"It's good?"

Nishell nodded. "Crazy good."

"Well then, I don't get a D-minus from you."

Nishell laughed. "No D-minus. Maybe a C-plus."

"You a hard grader," Jackson cracked.

For a couple of minutes, she ate contentedly. It was pleasant under the willow. A gentle breeze has started up. The food was brilliant. And Jackson was—was this possible?—even more gentle than the wind.

"I want to say something from my heart, 'cause I know you mad at me," Jackson told her when he saw she was halfway through her food.

"You gonna say you acted like a jerk last week after I told you what I told you?" Nishell asked. "It's true. You were a jerk to me; you were a jerk to Kiki Butler, and you were a jerk to her man, Sean—you practically killed him on the basketball court, and he your cousin!"

"I thought you were bein' unfair," Jackson stated carefully.

She drank some of the tea. "Because I said we couldn't do the deed till you started makin' yourself some grades?"

"You know it. My grades be my business, not yours."

Nishell shook her head. "No, Jackson. If you gonna be my man, they also be my business. I think you forget I was homeless, once upon a time. No way I let you end up the same way."

Jackson held the cold tea bottle against the back of his neck. "Day-um, Nishell! I ain't gonna be homeless."

"Tell me that when you don't get your diploma next year, and your mama toss you outta your house like my grand-parents tossed out my mom," Nishell declared.

"That was different," Jackson main-tained. He brushed his hand at a stray yellow jacket that was flitting around the picnic basket.

Nishell shook her head. "Not so much. Anyway, we can hang if you want. Just don't be 'spectin' nothing from me till you shape it up. Plus you owe Kiki Butler and your cousin a big-ass apology."

Jackson nodded. "Maybe I'll see 'em at Mio's tonight."

Mio's was the local pizza joint that was the unofficial headquarters of the yearbook club of South Central High School. Both Nishell and Jackson had been YC members last year. Nishell's friend Sherise—Kiki Butler's olderby-two-minutes twin sister—had been president of that club, and Nishell was the main photographer. Jackson hadn't joined YC by choice. He was forced there after he'd cut class one too many times.

When they finished their food and drinks, Nishell asked if they could walk down to the river so she could take a few pictures. A summer thunderstorm was moving in from the west. The storm was still many miles away, but sunlight streaked through thick clouds, playing on the buildings across the water. "It's gorgeous light."

Jackson grinned slyly. "Not as gorgeous as you. Course, I can't do anything but hold your hand now."

"Then hold it good." Nishell found her camera; Jackson helped her to her feet. Then she and Jackson walked hand-in-hand down the hill. It felt natural. Right. In fact, it felt so right that Nishell was tempted to break her own rules right then and there.

No. Do not do that.

She didn't. Instead, she posed Jackson artfully by the railing, looking out at the water. The ochre sunlight made his muscles look extra buff. He had amazing guns.

Click. Click, click, click. She snapped off four shots. Then four more.

"Don't move," she told him. She moved in for some close-ups. *Click, click.* Two from the side. *Click, click.* Then two from behind.

"You're doin' great," she told him. "Just don't—hey!—ow!"

Something slammed into her so hard from behind that she lost her balance and rammed into Jackson. He fell to the ground; she threw out her hands to break her own fall.

"What the hell?!" Jackson exclaimed.

If it hadn't been for the low iron railing that separated the path from the water, they both would have had an unplanned swim. Nishell looked to see what had smacked her. She spotted it immediately, overturned on the ground. A runaway baby carriage.

Oh no! Is there a baby?

"Oh my God, I am so, so sorry!" A young woman with an infant in her arms came running down the hill toward them. "Are you guys okay? I stopped to get her bottle and the carriage got away!"

"We're fine," Nishell assured, relieved that the baby was safe.

"Good thing your kid wasn't in it," Jackson told the woman. He retrieved the carriage and got it upright. It seemed functional.

"Next time, I'm settin' the brake." The young mother put her baby in the carriage. "All right, see you guys!"

With a little wave, she headed out.

"All right, see you guys!" Jackson imitated in a high voice once the woman was out of earshot. "I almost put you both in the river, see you guys!"

Nishell laughed. Then she froze.

"Jackson?"

"Yeah?"

She scanned the blacktop near them. Nothing.

Oh no. Please no. Please, please, please! Where is it?

"Have you ... have you seen my camera?"

Jackson cursed under his breath. He knew that Nishell's camera was her most prized possession. She'd worked a whole year after school serving ice cream to buy it—over her mother's objections.

The two of them scoured the area carefully. No camera.

"Umm, Nishell?" Jackson was looking over the side of the railing.

"Uh-huh?"

Jackson pointed.

Nishell followed his gaze. The camera was perched on a rock embankment, down by the water's edge. Nishell realized it must have gone through the railing when she fell. It looked okay, though.

"No worries. I got it covered," Jackson announced.

He scrambled over the railing to climb down and retrieve it. Just as he did, a speedboat roared past them upstream, kicking up a huge wake. To Nishell's horror, the wave rolled toward the bank and engulfed the embankment.

When it washed back out, the camera was gone.

I can't believe my camera drowned!" Nishell moaned as she and Jackson got close to the door of Mio's.

"You'll get another one," Jackson assured her.

"How? I'm too old for the Tooth Fairy."

It was three hours later. Sherise Butler had called an odd summer meeting of the yearbook club, to be held at Mio's. Once she and Jackson were inside, Nishell could see that everyone had shown up. She even spotted the year-book club advisor, language arts teacher Ms. Okoro. It was funny to see that she still dressed like a teacher even though it was summer vacation. She wore a conservative black skirt and flowing orange top, with a lot of jewelry from her native Nigeria.

Kiki Butler stood with Marnyke Cooper, who looked typically fly in a short red dress and very high black heels. As for Kiki, she was in her usual basketball kicks, red basketball shorts, and a cutoff T-shirt. By herself near the counter was Tia Ramirez, second in command to Sherise at YC. Tia wore Tia-casual, which meant ironed jeans and a black long-sleeve cotton shirt.

Jackson immediately peeled off to join his homeboys in the back—Carlos Howard, Lattrell Chance, and Sean King. Carlos was Sherise's boyfriend. Lattrell was Jackson's best homeboy. And Sean was Kiki's man as well as Jackson's cousin. Nishell watched Jackson go to

Sean and take him aside. That he made everything straight was obvious from how the guys embraced afterward.

"That's good," Nishell thought. "Now he just gotta do the same to Kiki. Without the hug!"

"I see your man makin' the rounds." Sherise sidled over to join Nishell. Sherise's summer job was at a clothing store at the Eastside Mall, and she always looked sharp. Tonight she wore a short pink skirt and a black top.

"He got a lot to make up for," Nishell quipped.

"Honestly, Nish. I don't know how you can put up wit' him."

Nishell raised the corners of her mouth in a half-smile, as she saw Jackson now talking earnestly with Kiki. She was nodding as he spoke. Obviously, he was apologizing to her too. "That a good question. But I find a way."

Sherise lowered her voice. "How he doin' wit' yo' wrench?"

"My what?" Then Nishell laughed. "Oh! You mean the wrench I'm keepin' closed!"

"No, I mean the wrench that's fixin' your toilet—of course the one you keepin' closed!"

"So far, so good. He made me a picnic today down by the river."

Sherise sniffed. "Don't get it twisted; he tryin' to charm you. Check with me in a week." She looked around the brightly lit pizza joint with its bolted-down orange Formica tables and plastic chairs. "I guess everyone's here. Let's start."

"What's this meeting for, anyway?" Nishell asked.

Sherise smiled slyly. "You'll see. So will Tia." She picked up a knife and a water glass and tapped the knife against the glass. "Come on, everyone. Gather round, gather round! Pizza and drinks afterward, on me. Thank you, Mio, for turnin' down the music! And thanks for having us."

The boss turned down the hip-hop and gave a little wave. There were a lot of cheap food places on Twenty-Third Street, but the YC kids always seemed to end up at Mio's joint. The lights were harsh, and the décor hadn't changed since Mio's grandpa had opened the place way back when. Still, the pizza was cheap and good, and Mio stayed cool when things got loud and rowdy. He hadn't even called the cops when Jackson and Sean had nearly come to blows a couple of weeks back.

Everyone slid their plastic chairs over to where Sherise stood. Ms. O waited discreetly off to one side. Nishell knew that her policy was to let the kids run yearbook meetings, unless there was a good reason for her to step in.

"Well, here we are," Sherise said. "School's out and I'm not big on speeches, so I'll keep this short. We got nominated for that best-in-state award this past spring, but we didn't win. Next year, I want to win."

"That means you gotta actually do some work, Sherise!" Jackson hooted. "And not let Tia do it all!"

The group cracked up. Sherise had beaten Tia for yearbook president and then appointed Tia yearbook manager. It was well-known that Tia did most of the heavy lifting while Sherise got most of the glory.

"If I was you, Jackson," Sherise shot back, "I'd worry more about the school-work you need to be doin' and less about what I got to be doin'."

People laughed again, louder this time. Everyone knew about Jackson's academic issues.

"If we're gonna win, we're gonna have to take it to the next level," Sherise told them. "We already got a website. I want to keep it active all summer. Then next year we'll do a section in the print year-book about this summer."

"What's that mean for us?" Marnyke asked cautiously.

"It means I need everyone to get out there in the hood. See what people are doin' for the summer and write it up or take pictures. See who's workin' and who's playin' ball. Who's hittin' it with who. And who ain't hittin' it with who."

"Jackson, she talkin' about you!" Lattrell catcalled to a new wave of laughter. Nishell felt a little embarrassed. What she was doing with Jackson was supposed to be private. Instead, it seemed like everyone knew. She was trying to make a point, not humiliate her man.

Tia marched forward to stand by Sherise. "I think this is a great idea. We can divide into teams and contact every single kid in the senior class. I'll make a spreadsheet, and we can set up a database. I'll coordinate this whole thing."

"You would," someone muttered.

Nishell saw Kiki scowl at Tia. Kiki and Tia were tied for the highest grade point average in the school. Whoever finished next year with the best GPA would get an amazing scholarship that paid all their college expenses, including tuition. If they tied, they'd split the scholarship.

Kiki told me that she offered to team up with Tia so they'd be sure of sharing the scholarship, and Tia told her to go to hell. I'd scowl too.

I wonder what Sherise thinks of all that.

She got her answer a moment later.

—

"I don't think that's necessary, Tia," Sherise said lightly. "Kiki, can you join me?"

With a bitter glance at Tia, Kiki stepped up next to her sister.

"I'm making a change," Sherise declared. "I want everyone to meet the new yearbook club manager, Kiki Butler. Give it up for Kiki Butler!"

Whoa baby!

There was healthy clapping and hooting from everyone except Tia, who fumed. She was as icy as liquid nitrogen, and she confronted Sherise right in front of everyone.

"I'm the manager, Sherise. You can't do that."

Sherise grinned coldly. "I just did."

Tia swung around toward Ms. O. "Tell her she can't, Ms. O. I worked my butt off last year. I'm going to run for YC president again in the fall. She's doing this to help her sister. It's not fair."

Kiki spoke up, with an edge to her voice. "Last time I looked, Sherise was president. That means she can hand out the jobs." She glared again at Tia. "You can always bail on yearbook, you know."

Tia glared at her. "I don't bail. Period."

"Well," Ms. O hedged. "I'm afraid Sherise and Kiki are right. Sherise is in charge until the next election. It's her decision, Tia. I'm not saying I agree with it."

"Do you?" Tia pressed. "Do you?"

"Take a chill pill, girl!" Lattrell called out.

"Whether I agree doesn't matter," Ms. O told her. "I'm the advisor here. You guys need to solve this on your own."

"Thank you, Ms. O," Sherise said to her. "Congratulations, Kiki. Guys, check in with my sister on your work. Take lots of pictures too. Now get yourselves some pizza!"

The meeting broke up, and Nishell slid over to Sherise. The two of them had gotten to be pretty good friends the last couple of months of school, but Tia had once been a good friend too. Maybe not as much recently as back in the fall or winter, but friendships were sometimes like that.

Nishell didn't like how Tia had treated Kiki, but she didn't like how Sherise was treating Tia, either. Tia had it diagnosed right. It was a blatant power play.

"That was harsh," Nishell told Sherise.

Sherise shrugged. "Whatever."

"You did that just to help your sister."

Sherise shook her head. "Well, not just to help Kiki. To hurt Tia. She better recognize."

"You admit it?" Nishell was astonished.

"Hey, it was too tempting to resist. What'd she think was going to happen? Now, you in or not?"

"What do mean?" Nishell was puzzled.

"I mean, are you in on the summer project or not?"

"I'm in," she told Sherise.

"Good. We're gonna need a lot of photographs."

Nishell saw Tia listening in. It didn't really matter.

"I'm ready to take as many pics as you want," Nishell told Sherise. "But I'm gonna need a camera."

"What happened to yours?" Sherise asked.

"It's at the bottom of the river." Nishell told her the story of what had happened with the baby carriage and Jackson that afternoon.

Sherise whistled. "Let me see what I can do."

Nishell nodded. "Let's all see what we can do. Unless you want me to just shoot 'em on my cell phone."

"That wouldn't be good," Tia commented.

Sherise stared at her. "Did I ask you, Tia?"

Nishell frowned. This was no way for Sherise to treat someone who'd worked so hard on the yearbook.

In fact, it was wrong. Very, very wrong.

CHAPTER

3

Nishell saw her mother, Sierra, look at the kitchen wall clock and frown. "Just a sec, Nishell," she said. Then she cupped her hands and yelled toward the back of the house. "Ka'lon? Get a move on! You don't want to be late for camp!"

Ka'lon hollered back at her. "I'm coming! I'm coming!"

Indeed, he was. Clad in a gray camp shorts and a matching gray "Fresh Air Camper!" T-shirt, with white socks on his feet, Ka'lon roared out of his bedroom, through the small living room, and skidded on his stocking feet across the kitchen floor. Though he was compact and solidly built, he came to a perfect stop and plopped into his seat at the small round table like he'd done it a hundred times. Actually, he had.

It was nine the next morning. Ka'lon—Sierra had sort of named him for Superman's name back when he was a baby on the planet Krypton—was due on the Fresh Air Camp bus at nine thirty. That bus was taking him and forty other campers upstate, where Ka'lon would spend the next two weeks playing games, hunting for frogs, and having a good old time.

It would be Ka'lon's first time away from home. Nishell was a little nervous for him. Sierra was even more on edge.

"Eat something, Ka'lon," Sierra commanded. She was dressed for work at the homeless shelter, where she answered phones and served as a resource person.

Sierra was white, with gray eyes and stocky legs. She still wore her long brunette hair in a girlish ponytail. Nishell knew she could be pretty if she did something with her hair and put on some makeup, but she had that all-natural thing happening.

Ka'lon winked at Nishell. "Okay, Mom. I want a Big Mac, fries, and a vanilla shake."

"Not funny," Sierra told him. She was no-nonsense this morning. "Cereal."

"Okay. Frosty Flakes with Frosty Milk."

"What's Frosty Milk?" Sierra asked.

Ka'lon had a sense of humor almost as good as Jackson's. "Sugar."

Nishell laughed. She was going to miss her little brother. He was lucky. She'd never gone to any kind of camp. When she'd been his age, she and Sierra had lived at the Tenth Street homeless shelter—where her mom now worked. By the time Ka'lon came along, Sierra had been able to save enough money to rent the home they were in now.

As Ka'lon poured a bowl of cereal and topped it with milk, Nishell took in her familiar surroundings. Their rental was one story, on a tough block. There was a gang house three doors to the east, and a couple of other homes were boarded up. They had a kitchen, a living room, and two bedrooms. Ka'lon had a bedroom, and Nishell had a bedroom. Sierra slept on a pull-out couch.

Ka'lon ate quickly, then he went to get his small backpack. Sierra sighed when he was gone. "His camp sure is different from my camp," she said with a touch of bitterness.

"Where'd you go?" Nishell queried.

"A place in Maine called Mataponi." Sierra got a far-off look in her eyes. "We had horses and sailboats. There was even a playhouse for musicals. Kids came from all over the world to go there."

"How much did it cost?" Nishell asked curiously. Her mom hadn't talked about her girlhood in a long time.

"You really want to know?" There was that bitter tone again.

Nishell nodded.

"I looked it up on the Internet last week," Sierra confessed. "If I were to send you this summer? It's more than ten thousand dollars. For seven weeks."

"Ten thousand dollars!" Nishell sputtered. "Where did you guys sleep? In a palace?"

Sierra shook her head. "Just bunks. My parents were rich. They still are."

"Too bad they cut you off," Nishell told her. "We might be living in a place where you could have an actual bedroom of your own. You know, I could sleep on the couch next year."

Sierra's eyes hardened. Nishell didn't know much about her grandparents, even though they lived just ten miles away in Majestic Oaks, one of the city's nicest suburbs. It might as well have been ten light years. They sent an annual Christmas card, so Nishell knew what they looked like. Other than that, she knew practically nothing. Sierra barely talked about them.

"I don't want their money," Sierra muttered.

"They cut you off when you were pregnant with me," Nishell recalled. "Because my father was black."

"Something like that," Sierra agreed.

"That's messed up."

Sierra took a long, thoughtful sip of coffee. "I agree. I'm their kid. But to cut off you and Ka'lon too? That's what I find inexcusable."

"What's their excuse?" Nishell asked.

Sierra shrugged. "Maybe seeing you guys reminds them of me. I was a Mataponi girl. Mataponi girls don't get pregnant by boys from the hood." She cupped her hands again and turned back toward Ka'lon's bedroom, where he had disappeared again after gulping down his breakfast. "Ka'lon! Get a move on!"

"Here I come!"

Once again, Ka'lon made his grand entrance. As he put his sneakers on, Nishell found a disposable camera her mom had bought at the dollar store and stuck in a drawer. She took a couple of shots of Ka'lon, and then she pressed the lousy camera into his hands.

If only my camera hadn't ended up in the river.

"Fill this with pictures of your friends," she told him.

"I'll fill it with pictures of Frosty Flakes," he promised. Then he put his arms out wide for a hug. Nishell embraced him.

"See you in two weeks," Nishell murmured. "Be careful. And stay out of poison ivy!" She followed him and Sierra to the door. One more big hug and Ka'lon was gone. Nishell sighed when the door closed. Two weeks of peace, but she sure was going to miss him.

She was still in her bathrobe; she had to shower and dress before she went to the day-care center. She was on her way to the bathroom when she heard the front doorbell ring.

Huh? They must have forgotten something.

She tightened her robe, then hurried to the door and opened it, expecting to see a harried Sierra and her brother. Instead, there was a FedEx guy in a uniform, with a white delivery truck parked out on the street behind him.

"Nishell Saunders?"

"That's me," she responded, surprised.

He thrust a clipboard at her. "For you. Sign here."

She signed. He handed her a box, then trotted away.

Who's sending me a FedEx?

There was no return address. She went inside and closed the door before she opened it.

"Holy moly!" she exclaimed. "Holy moly, holy moly! Who sent me this?"

It was a new digital camera. Not just any digital camera either—but a Leica V-Lux with a super-telephoto zoom lens. Made in Germany, it was just about the finest digital camera money could buy. Nishell had coveted one, forever.

Who sent this to her? It had to be Sierra. That was amazing. Even with Ka'lon going off to camp, her mother had managed to scrape together the money, order it, and have it delivered the next day.

She owed her mom the biggest thank you in human history.

Once Nishell's heart stopped—well, sort of stopped—pounding, she pressed speed dial on her cell. Nishell was so grateful. Her mother actually thought the whole photography thing was a waste of time. Usually, Sierra was on Nishell's case to be a nurse or a dental tech.

"You know, Nishell," she'd always say, "a job where you'd actually make some decent money."

"Nishell, make it quick!" her mother answered. "We're at the bus; it's a madhouse!"

"You should have given me the camera before he left," Nishell joshed. "I could be right there with you, shooting the whole thing for his memory box."

There was a moment's silence. Then her mother asked what Nishell was talking about.

"The camera. It came by FedEx this morning!"

"Nishell, if someone got you a camera, it wasn't me. If I were you, I'd ask Jackson. Bet he feels guilty you lost your other one. Okay, gotta go. Ka'lon's waving!" Her mother clicked off.

Whoa. It hadn't been her mother. If not Sierra, then who?

Nishell decided to take her mother's advice and call Jackson. He didn't answer. That was strange. As far as Nishell knew, he wasn't working. She wondered if he was out looking for a job. She sent him a text.

Boo—Was it u? Call me!

Three hours later, Nishell and her new camera were the hit of the day-care.

She'd spent an hour at home reading the owner's manual and figuring out some basic functions, and then showed up with the Leica around her neck. She quickly snapped a few candid shots of kids having a tug-of-war. When Mrs. Phillips, the woman who ran the day-care, came over and saw the results, she quickly put Nishell to work.

"Can you take some more, then print 'em out on my printer and make a photo board for the parents to see?" she asked. "They're always wanting pictures of their kids, and I never have any."

"I can do that easy," Nishell promised.

"Then you're off kid duty and on camera duty."

"Yes, ma'am!" Nishell loved the idea. She'd get to practice with her new toy.

She spotted two little girls holding hands, playing a counting game. *Click.*

Three boys crashing tricycles into each other, and laughing at the results. *Click.*

A girl poking at an anthill in the dirt. *Click.*

A bunch of kids inhaling Fudgesicles, their faces covered in chocolate. *Click, click, click, click.*

Then as naptime approached, Nishell spotted Tia—who was also working at the day-care—tucking in a couple of kids. She was about to photograph the scene when her cell sounded. She checked caller ID.

Jackson! Finally!

"Hey, Baby," he said after she'd answered. "I got your text. Whatchu talkin' about, was it me?"

Nishell thought Jackson was kidding around.

"Oh," she said, "I just might have gotten a visit from the FedEx dude this morning, and he might have brought me a package, and in that package might have been this bangin' camera that I got round my neck at this very moment. Was it you?"

"Nah," Jackson confessed. "I wish I could say it was. But it wasn't."

"Oh."

The mystery had just gotten deeper.

"You don't know who sent it?"

"Nope."

"Well, when you got it figured out, tell that person to send me one too. Not one. A dozen. I'll sell 'em on eBay and take you to Hawaii. Anyway, I'm glad you texted. Whatchu doin' tomorrow night?" Jackson asked.

"I don't know. I think I'm about to spend it with you."

Jackson laughed. "I'd like that."

"Not horizontal, Jackson," Nishell warned. "No matter how much I like you."

"Nah. Not horizontal, not standing. Sitting. I'm taking you out."

"Where?" Nishell asked, as she saw Tia finishing with the kids. "And how come it ain't tonight?"

—

Jackson chuckled. "I'm stayin' in and bein' good tonight. Tomorrow? That's a surprise. I'll check in with you later."

"Later, Boo," Nishell said.

Before she went back to work, Nishell quickly called everyone else she thought might have something to do with the camera. Ms. Okoro. Sherise. Even Kiki. No luck. It was as much a mystery as ever.

For the next half-hour, Nishell took some shots of counselors drinking sodas or preparing for the afternoon onslaught after the little kids woke up. She passed Tia, sitting alone on one of the playground swings, and remembered what Sherise had said about the summer YC project. If she could talk to Tia and maybe even photograph her, she could do double duty.

"Hey, Tia, what's up?"

"Hey yourself. Nice camera."

"Thanks. Someone sent it to me. My other one ended up in the river yesterday."

"I heard you talking about that. You like this one?"

"I love it! You mind if I take some shots of you? For Mrs. Phillips and the yearbook?"

Tia shrugged. "Suit yourself. Not that I care about yearbook anymore."

"After last night, you mean?" Nishell took a few pictures of Tia on the swing, thinking how she looked younger and gentler than the tough image she presented.

"Exactly. Mind you, if Sherise and Kiki think I'm going let them walk all over me, they're in for a surprise."

"What are you planning?"

"I'm not sure," Tia admitted. "But I'll tell you what, and I don't care if Kiki and Sherise know this or not. I'm already doing the reading for next year. I'm doing the math. I speak Spanish and English, so I'm starting French on my computer. Once I have that down, I'll start Japanese. If Kiki thinks she has a chance at that scholarship instead of me, she's dead wrong."

"Why are you telling me all this?" Nishell challenged. "I hang with Kiki and Sherise sometimes."

Tia smiled. "You think I don't know that? Go ahead and tell them. Kiki doesn't scare me."

"Maybe not. But you don't sound like you're having much fun," Nishell responded.

"I'll have fun when I'm at Harvard," was Tia's terse response as she looked into the camera with grim determination.

"So tell me about a typical day," Nishell prompted. "For the yearbook."

"Sure. I'm up at four and in my parents' bakery by five," Tia reported. "I help with the baking, and then we open at six. I work the counter until ten fifteen. Then I'm here at day-care from eleven to six. After work, I go home, eat, and study until eleven. Then I go to bed."

Nishell winced. That was brutal. "What about weekends?"

"What are those?" Tia cracked.

The two girls laughed. Nishell understood that Kiki was going to have to bring her A-plus game if she was going to have any chance at the all-expenses-paid scholarship. Tia wasn't holding anything back.

"I don't know how I feel about all this," Nishell thought. "I like Sherise a lot. I like Kiki. But I don't respect them like I do Tia, even if she can be a bee-yotch when there's something she wants."

"You don't know how it was for me in Mexico," Tia confided.

"You don't know how it was for me when I was little, either." Nishell said, thinking about her childhood at the homeless shelter.

"Actually, I do. You talked about it at the school assembly; how you used to not have a place to live," Tia reminded. She leaned forward and pressed her chin into her hands.

"That's not the whole story."

Nishell fired off a last couple of pictures, thinking that no one would ever call Tia a babe. Her personality was just too strong. But she was beautiful, with her dark eyes, thick dark hair, and glasses that made her look like a college student already.

"I know enough," Tia told her.

Sparkling chimes sounded, indicating the end of rest period and back to work for the staff. Nishell thanked Tia and spent the rest of the afternoon in Mrs. Phillips's small office. After uploading the photos to the computer, it was easy to pick several dozen to print, and then make them into a collage. By the time the kids were ready to be picked up, Nishell had mounted the collage on a poster for the adults to admire.

Admire it they did.

"You did great," Mrs. Phillips told her after everyone had filed out. "I still want you to work with the kids, but if we need you to take more pictures, can you? You can be the official photographer."

"I'd love to," Nishell said sincerely. She felt like she was on top of the world.

Official day-care photographer. Okay. It's not shootin' fashion for Ebony. *But it ain't bad.*

Nishell said good-bye to Mrs. Phillips and headed out, trying to figure out what to do with her evening. She decided to stay home and learn everything she could about her new camera.

"Nishell Saunders?"

Nishell looked up. Parked at the curb not far from the day-care was a white BMW. Standing outside the Beemer was a white woman in her late 50s or early 60s. She had short brown hair and wore khaki trousers, a checked-print blouse made of silk, and brown pumps.

No. It can't be.

It is.

"Nishell? Do you know who I am?"

Nishell gulped. She did know who this was. She recognized the woman from the annual Christmas card.

This was her grandmother.

One hour later, Nishell sat in a daze across from her grandparents in the nicest restaurant at the nicest hotel in the city, the Hotel San Marino. They were at a small round table tucked discreetly in the back. She wore the same clothes she had on at the day-care. Her grandmother had offered to stop and buy her a dress and new shoes, but Nishell had said no way.

"They got to take me as I am, if they take me at all," Nishell told herself, as a waiter, dressed in black with a white towel draped artfully over one arm, took their orders. She literally pinched her own arm to make sure she wasn't dreaming. Or that she hadn't stepped into a weird parallel universe where she and her mother's parents had a real relationship.

I'm having an actual meal with my grandparents.

She studied her grandfather as he ordered for all of them. Steak for him, roast monkfish—whatever that was!—for her grandmother, and lobster ravioli for Nishell. He looked like how a white grandfather was supposed to look. Tall and thin, with thick white hair and a white moustache. He wore a white shirt, a beige sport jacket, and tan trousers.

When they'd surprised her at the day-care, she'd hesitated before getting in their car. Going with her grandparents felt disloyal. She'd even called her mother. To her surprise, Sierra was okay with it. "This day was going to come sometime,"

Sierra had said. "I guess sometime is today. I won't be home till late tonight. We'll talk about it in the morning."

The ride to the hotel had been quiet. Nishell had so many things she wanted to ask them and so much anger to express about how they'd treated her mother and her. But the few sentences they'd exchanged had been about what names Nishell should use with them. Her grandparents had asked her to call them "Grandma" and "Grandpa." Nishell had said she wasn't ready for that. Their names were Carla and Dave. That's what she wanted to use.

"Carla and Dave are fine," Carla assured her. "I hope that will change."

Once orders were taken, water poured, and martinis brought for both Carla and Dave, Carla raised her glass. "I suppose a toast is in order. Here's to life. Full of surprises."

Dave and Carla clinked glasses. Nishell lifted a water goblet in their direction, feeling incredibly confused. She hadn't seen her grandparents since she'd been a toddler. What could prompt them to come to her now?

"Hear, hear!" Dave exclaimed.

"This sure is a surprise," Nishell managed to say, trying to figure out the best time to lay into them with her questions.

"I imagine it is. Like the camera that arrived today," Carla said with a sly smile. "We figured you deserved to know who it was from."

"It was from you?"

"It was from us," Dave acknowledged. He had a kind voice. "We got a call from someone close to you—"

"Who? My mom? Sherise? Jackson? Kiki?" Nishell blurted. " 'Cause they all said—"

"I don't know any of those people, and I can assure you that it wasn't your mother," Carla responded through clenched teeth. "I don't think your mother would call us if aliens landed on your front lawn and demanded, 'Take me to your mother!'"

"Then who?" Nishell demanded.

Carla took a sip of her martini—Dave had ordered it straight up, with some fancy gin and a single olive. "I can't say. The person wanted to tell you at the appropriate time, if he or she so chooses."

Nishell slumped against the red velvet of her chair. "That's not much help."

Carla smiled thinly. "There are some mysteries in life that we just have to endure, dear. I certainly live with many unanswered questions," her voice trailed off. "If it bothers you too much, you can always give the camera back. That would be your choice, Nishell."

Give it back? Her grandparents must be nuts to think she'd give it back.

"You ain't got me nothin' since I was in diapers," Nishell said hotly. "I don't think I'm givin' this back."

"Nor should you," Carla said. It was obvious which grandparent did most of the talking. "It's yours. Oh look! Here come our appetizers. I love this restaurant. The chef is topnotch. You need to try everything."

The waiter was back with three small appetizer plates, explaining each dish as he placed it on the table. There were fresh-picked wild mushrooms sautéed in garlic sauce and topped with shaved truffles. There were hand-gathered steamed mussels plucked from their shells and nestled on shredded seaweed and butter lettuce, and there was a plate of baked French bread slices topped with melted cheese and more truffles.

Nishell had never eaten a truffle in her life. She wasn't about to start now. What if she hated it? She didn't want to have to force it down or spit it out in front of Dave and Carla. She tried one of the mussels instead. It was okay. Frankly, she liked fried shrimp a lot better. Meanwhile, she had some questions to ask her grandparents.

"Why now?" she asked.

Carla finished chewing a mouthful of mushrooms before she answered. "Why now, what?"

"Why now you contactin' me? After everything?" Nishell asked. She looked around the elegant restaurant. It was full of business people dining on expense accounts. She didn't see a single black face besides her own. Correction. There was one black busboy.

"When we got the call about the camera—don't ask me from who, please—

your grandfather and I had a serious discussion. Isn't that right, Dave?"

"It is, Carla," her grandfather confirmed. "A very serious discussion."

"Serious indeed," Carla repeated for the third time, which made Nishell doubt the truth of what she was saying. "We decided it has been too long. Whatever issues we had with your mother—and whatever issues we currently have with your mother—do not need to carry over to you and your younger brother."

"So you're askin' me to have a relationship with you, and you're askin' Ka'lon—who's at camp for two weeks—to have a relationship with you, but you don't want my mother to have a relationship with you. Do I have that right?" Nishell challenged. The mussels on the plate were getting cold, but she didn't care.

Carla took one more sip from her martini. "How old are you, Nishell?"

Nishell was one of the oldest kids heading into senior year at South Central High School. She'd started kindergarten at seven, after she and her mom had left the shelter.

"Eighteen," she said. "I turn nineteen in the fall."

"Eighteen." Carla smoothed away a non-existent wrinkle on the right sleeve of her blouse. "I'd say that's old enough to make your own decisions."

"Maybe," Nishell allowed. "But I need to know what happened with you and my mom."

Carla shook her head. "I disagree. This isn't about your mother and us. This is about you and your brother and us. We're offering an opportunity to rebuild a broken bridge. I would hope that your mother has raised you to be the kind of girl who'd want to do that."

Nishell was silent. She thought about eating more, but she drank a little water instead. What her grandmother was proposing was perfectly reasonable, true. Still, something about it seemed wrong.

"Can you do that?" Carla pressed.

Nishell stared at the woman a long time before she answered, searching for some hint of her own features in her grandmother's face. She didn't see any. In fact, if she didn't know that Carla was her grandmother, she'd never have been able to guess.

"I don't know if I can do it, Carla," Nishell told her honestly. "And even if I could do it? I don't know if I'd want to. What you did to my mother, to me and my brother? It was evil!"

CHAPTER
6

When Nishell came out of her room the next morning, she found a note from her mom on the kitchen table.

N—

Slept in Ka'lon's room. First night not on couch since he was a toddler! Had a date last night. Have set my alarm for 9:30 a.m. If you get up before me, go to the Fat Man. Will meet you there for breakfast. My treat. It's right by the day-care. I'll go to work from there.

I want to hear everything!

XO

Mom

Nishell grinned. Well, well, well. Her mother had a date. She'd have to find out what that was about, and she had a zillion things to say about her dinner with her grandparents. She was glad she was about to have a relaxed meal with her mom. Plus, the Fat Man was the bomb. It was a breakfast and soul food place on Twenty-Third near the intersection with King Memorial Drive. Famous for flapjacks and chitlins, Nishell had only eaten there a couple of times.

Maybe it's not so bad to have my little brother away at camp.

Forty-five minutes later, she'd washed up, dressed for work, slung on her camera, and took the bus to the stop just outside the Fat Man. She'd found a table for two—the place was busy even though it was a weekday—and ordered coffee and a doughnut. An old waitress named Geraldine scolded her choice of food.

A girl her age needed to eat healthy. Nishell didn't disagree. She changed her order to scrambled eggs and toast.

Geraldine grunted approval and hustled off to the kitchen. By the time she'd come back with coffee and a couple of waters, Nishell saw Sierra enter. She waved at her mother, who joined her. Her mom looked great. She wore a sleek black pantsuit and had even put on makeup.

"Wow," Nishell cracked. "You dressin' to impress?"

Sierra smiled sheepishly. "Maybe a little. The guy who took me out last night, Tony, he's doing a landscape job for the shelter."

Nishell scrunched up her face. "You're going out with a gardener?"

"If I was, what's it to you?" Sierra fired back.

Geraldine poured her some coffee, and Sierra quickly ordered eggs, grits, and bacon. Then she turned back to Nishell. "He happens to be a licensed landscape architect doing a charity project for the shelter. Don't be so quick to judge people, Nishell. Meanwhile, how was your field trip to the San Marino? My mother said it was—these are her words—'quite lovely.'"

"How do you know?" Nishell was astonished.

"She e-mailed me," Sierra said tonelessly. "Mostly because I'm sure she knew you would tell me, so she wanted to get in the first punch. Actually, it was the second punch. The first punch was that fancy camera."

"You don't like her very much," Nishell observed.

Sierra scowled. "She isn't very likeable. Of course, that's my opinion. What was the party line?"

"Excuse me?"

"What was the party line? What was her rap? What'd she say when you asked her why she hadn't contacted you since Bill Clinton was president? I know she did ninety percent of the talking. She always does ninety percent of the talking."

Geraldine brought their food; Nishell figured there must have been a small army cooking for it to come out of the kitchen that fast. She tasted the eggs. Light and fluffy, perfectly salted. This was a low-rent meal after the San Marino, but she liked it a whole lot better.

Nishell told the truth. There was no sense in lying. Things between her mother and her grandparents couldn't get any worse.

"I called her evil. She said that no matter how bad things were with you, there was no reason for them to be bad with me and Ka'lon."

"Exactly the right thing to say," Sierra said approvingly. Then she leaned toward Nishell and spoke fiercely. "Nishell, you're eighteen. You make your own decisions about this stuff. I sure would love for you and Ka'lon to have actual grandparents, since you sure don't have a daddy—and I've never forgiven myself for that. But I don't trust my mother. She's always got an agenda."

"I'll be careful," Nishell promised.

Sierra sighed. "You can't be careful enough. Nishell? Your grandmother is a lot like a restaurant, now that I think about it. Nothing is free. You want to eat? You pay."

I cannot believe it. I cannot believe Jackson Beauford took me here.

Nishell looked excitedly around the interior of Downtown Comedy, the most famous comedy club in the city. All wood paneled, with dozens of small round tables, the place was jammed with grownups and teens of all sizes and colors. On stage was a comedian she'd seen on BET who was finishing a routine about his manipulative mother.

"Me and my brother Ike and my mom, we were dangling out of a helicopter on a rope. Now, the rope couldn't hold us all," said the comedian. "An' we knew one of us had to let go so the rope wouldn't break. So my mom, she says, 'I am ready to die to save you both. I'm doing this for you, for your father, and for your futures. You especially, Ike. You mean everything to me!' And my brother Ike? What does he do? He applauds!"

The audience howled with glee and applauded. Nishell hooted and clapped too. She looked over at Jackson, who'd put on a white shirt and clean jeans for the evening. He was laughing so hard that tears were rolling down his face.

I am at Downtown Comedy on an actual date with Jackson Beauford. I must be dreaming.

Jackson had called her at work and said he had something special planned for the evening. She should look fly, and he'd pick her up. He'd even asked to borrow his mom's car so they didn't have to take the bus.

She chose her clothes carefully, putting on tight gray pants and a plunging silky black top that made Jackson grin. All the way downtown, Nishell pestered him good-naturedly about their destination. Jackson said it was a surprise.

It had been a fantastic surprise. They'd arrived in time for a light dinner of burger sliders and fries. Nishell had filled Jackson in on everything that had happened with her mom and grand-parents. Then came the comics, four of them. Each one funnier than the next.

Now the master of ceremonies was calling for quiet. She was a middle-aged black woman who looked more like a librarian than a comedienne, but she had actually opened the show with a side-splitting routine about a visit to the emergency room with the worst gas pains of her life.

"Well, well, as you know, it's time for a Downtown Comedy tradition," she announced. "Before our last act, we do a minute of open mike. Here's your chance to try out your best jokes on the toughest audience in the world. Who's up for it?"

"Open mike?" Nishell thought. "What could be more embarrassing? What person in their right mind—"

Oh no.

Jackson's hand wasn't just in the air. Both his hands were in the air, waving wildly.

The emcee spotted him right away. "Well, it look like we got a brother without a brain! Come on up here, brainless! What yo' name? Give it up for the brother without a brain!"

Nishell flushed, then clapped wildly as Jackson bounded up a short staircase to the stage. "Name's Jackson Beauford," he told her, borrowing her hand-held mike like a pro. "And you be right. I'm dumber than a sewer grate!"

The audience roared with laughter.

"Well, good luck, brother without a brain. Let's welcome Jackson Beauford to the Downtown Comedy stage!"

Jackson strutted to the center of the stage like he'd been doing stand-up his whole life.

"Hey, the emcee got it right," he told the audience. "I ain't got a brain to call my own. Just take a look at my report card. I'm a junior in high school, and I'm gonna be a junior in high school for the rest of my life if I can't get my grades up. I'm so bad at school that when they gave me my report card, they made me stand on a chair to read it, hopin' it would raise my IQ!"

The audience laughed appreciatively. Nishell beamed. If Jackson could be half as funny up on stage as he was in real life, he might make it through the two minutes without being ridiculed.

"Well, you'd think when I got home I'd catch hell from my mama," Jackson went on. "And I did. But it wasn't nothin' compared to what I caught from my girlfriend, Nishell. You see that gorgeous girl sittin' at that table by herself? That's her. Give a hand!"

The audience cheered; Nishell gave a shy little wave. When the crowd quieted, Jackson continued. "I mean it. Nishell be tough. If President Obama gets the kind of hell from Michelle when he messes up that I got from Nishell, there might not be much linkin' in the Lincoln bedroom, if you know what I'm sayin'!"

Once again, the audience cracked up. In any other circumstance, Nishell would have been mortified. Embarrassed. Hiding under the table. Tonight, though? It was somehow okay, because Jackson was actually making fun of himself.

"Here's what Nishell said to me. She said, 'Jackson, you make grades like that? You gotta answer to your mama. And since it don't seem like your mama can move you, I bet I can. An' I can do it by not movin' for you. If you know what

I'm sayin'.' Can you brothers dig it? She cut me off!"

The guys in the crowd shouted and pumped their fists. The women and girls hooted with delight.

"How many men think that be a good idea?" Jackson asked.

Silence.

"How many ladies?"

The female half of the audience went wild.

"Homeboys, I guess I just ruined your lives! Thank you! Good night!"

Jackson took a big bow, and the crowd got even louder. The emcee bounded out and took the mike from him. "Ladies and gentleman, Jackson Beauford, the brother without a brain, who just proved he has one! Thank you!"

Jackson bowed again and then jumped down from the stage. Nishell stood and embraced him, and the crowd cranked it up two more notches.

"How'd I do?" he murmured into her hair.

"You killed!"

She hugged him. He was handsome. He'd set up an amazing date. And most of all, he was funny.

She realized it was going to be very hard not to hit it with Jackson tonight.

CHAPTER

7

As Nishell had hoped, there was no one home when she and Jackson let themselves in her house.

"My mom's got another date," she told Jackson.

"You sure you want to do this?" he asked, as Nishell closed the door behind her.

She was sure. Jackson had been so wonderful tonight. He'd been a gentleman. And when he'd gotten up on that stage and made all those people laugh, it just about melted Nishell's heart into a big pool called "I want Jackson."

She reached up, snaked her arms sexily around his neck, and kissed him. The kiss was wonderful. Deep, sensual—it seemed to go on forever.

"Come to my room," she whispered.

"We're already there."

It was true. They'd somehow moved to the bedroom. She unbuttoned the top button of his shirt. He put his hands under her—

Boo-boop! Boo-boop!

Nishell's eyes snapped open as her phone sounded with an incoming text.

"Day-um. That was some dream," she muttered as she reached for her phone and noted the time. Ten twenty. She'd slept late. Really, really late. At least she had the day off from the day-care.

The text was from her mom.

Are you awake? I didn't want to awaken you.

Nishell smiled. It was so like her mother to text in complete sentences, with perfect spelling. She texted right back—in her own style.

> U were my alarm. Had gr8 nite w Jksn. Deets later!

Nishell stretched like a cat, happy in her memory of the night before. She'd already decided how to start her day. She'd interview Kiki for the YC project. Kiki had set up a tutoring business in the community room at Northeast Towers, and Nishell thought that shooting Kiki in action would make good pictures. Besides, she wanted to know what Kiki was doing to keep up with Tia in the battle for the Big Boss Scholarship.

After that, maybe I'll wander around downtown with my camera.

Nishell showered, put on a simple yellow sundress and sandals, and made herself a banana smoothie. She saw a notebook, envelopes, and stamps on the kitchen table. Her mother had obviously been writing a letter to Ka'lon. Nishell decided to write one too. But what to say? Should she mention their grand-parents?

Nah. TMI.

Nishell kept it real.

Hi Baby Bro,

Hope you're having a banging time at camp and not scaring your counselors too much. Everything here is good, but everyone misses you. I got a new camera to replace the one that went in the river, and I can't wait to take some pix of you with it when you come home. Be good and know that we miss you a lot. If you see a bear in the woods, run!

Love, Big Sis

She tore off the paper and got the letter ready to mail. On her way to the bus stop she dropped it in a mailbox. It was hard to believe that something as easy as writing a letter to her kid brother away at camp could make her feel so good. When the bus came, she took the steps two at a time.

It was amazing. On a budget of almost zero dollars, Kiki had remade one corner of the Northeast Towers community room into a classroom. Plastic milk crates were seats for the kids. Instead of whiteboards, Kiki used simple easels with poster board. There was a bookshelf with old picture books the library was giving away and a few donated rugs.

Kiki proudly showed it off, as two of her young students sprawled on rugs, reading simple chapter books. Meanwhile, Nishell took pictures of everything.

"All this happened because some kid's mother asked you to be her tutor?" Nishell marveled.

"Geneva." Kiki pointed at one of the girls—a skinny girl with her hair in braids sort of like Kiki's own.

"Who's the other one?" Nishell asked, then clicked off a couple of pictures.

"Geneva's bestie, Lawanda."

"How much you makin', if you don't mind?"

Kiki lowered her voice. "More than I ever thought I'd make, that's for sure." She motioned for Nishell to follow her; they sat on a couple of milk crates furthest from the kids. "You really want to know?"

Nishell nodded. She really did.

"Thirty-five an hour for two kids," Kiki confided. "Now mind you, that's not eight hours a day. In fact, I'm finishing with these two soon. Then I'm going to the ballgame with Sean, Marnyke, and her man, Gabe. I charge twenty an hour for one kid, and thirty-five for two."

Nishell did the math.

"Day-um, Kiki."

Kiki nodded. "I know. I'm doing a hundred a day, some days. If I did a bunch of advertisin' and really got the word out, I could be rakin' it in. Make more than my mom or stepdad, that's for sure."

"That's ... amazing."

"I know. I have to tell you, it's tempting just to let Tia win the scholarship and go to college here in town. I could keep up my business. By the time I was done with school, I'd have a whole lotta chip."

A couple of young women appeared at the door. Kiki waved to them.

"Excuse me, I gotta deliver these kids," she told Nishell.

"Do whatchu gotta do," Nishell said.

Nishell watched as Kiki got the two girls—they were so into their reading they hadn't even realized their moms had arrived—and walked them to the door. Cash changed hands. Then the kids and grownups were gone.

Kiki started back. But before she could even make it all the way across the stained floor, her boyfriend, Sean Ware, arrived, along with Marnyke Cooper and Marnyke's boyfriend, Gabe something-or-other. Nishell knew tall, skinny Sean. Marnyke was notorious as the class flirt. This was the first time she was meeting this Gabe guy. All she knew about him was that he was super-rich and came from Majestic Oaks, the same town where her grandparents lived. Marnyke had blabbed all about it. She'd met him a couple of weeks before.

Kiki made the introductions. Gabe was handsome for a white boy, with short brown hair, a scruffy beard, and green eyes. He was dressed in jeans and a T-shirt, as was Sean. Marnyke, though, wore heels and a tight white dress with diamond cutouts on both sides.

"God help her if someone bump her with a hot dog," Nishell thought. "She'll get mustard in places where it shouldn't be."

"You oughta come hear Gabe's band play sometime," Marnyke urged Nishell, then gazed at Gabe with adoration.

"I'm not sure I play Nishell's music," Gabe protested good-naturedly. "It sure wasn't Kiki and Sean's music when they came to hear me!"

"Well, there's a difference between Nishell and them," Marnyke told him.

"What's that?" Gabe asked.

"Nishell got taste," Marnyke declared.

Everyone laughed. Then Sean offered to take Gabe on a tour of the Northeast Towers projects.

"Not that there's much to see," he admitted.

"Sometimes college kids run ball on the basketball court," Nishell suggested. She wanted a few minutes alone with Kiki and Marnyke.

That was good enough for Gabe. "We'll be back when we're back," he told them, then took off with Sean.

Nishell waited for the guys to be gone before she turned to Kiki and Marnyke. "Can I ask you homegirls something?"

"Sure, anything," Kiki responded. Marnyke nodded agreement.

"I know this is trippin', but did either of you have anything to do with me gettin' this new camera?"

Nishell got all the answer she needed from her friends' puzzled looks.

"Nope," Kiki said anyway.

"Me neither," Marnyke told her. "How come you asking?"

Nishell shook her head. "It's not important. Anyway, your Gabe seem nice," she told Marnyke.

"He everything," Marnyke stated. "And that's with his clothes on. With his clothes off? He more than everything!"

Kiki and Nishell giggled at this.

"You still got Jackson on the bench?" Marnyke asked.

Nishell winced. "Does the whole YC know?"

Kiki sat on one of the milk crates. "Only the peeps who matter."

"You mean, not Tia," Nishell surmised.

"Who's Tia?" Kiki cracked.

Nishell shrugged. "I interviewed her for YC, you know."

"You were supposed to check with me about that," Kiki told her.

Nishell moved to the milk crate closest to Kiki. "I'm checking in now. She's studying for the SATs and trying to learn French. Meanwhile, she's workin' at the day-care and reading all these books. If you're gonna beat her for the scholarship, it's gonna take a lot of work."

Kiki looked disgusted. "The girl be a machine. Excuse me. I'm goin' to the bathroom. Whenever I hear Tia's name, I feel like I gotta puke."

"Girlfriend a little unnerved," Nishell observed as Kiki stomped away.

"If you were taking on the Bionic Latina, you'd be unnerved too," Marnyke quipped. "Maybe Kiki's so into this tutoring thing because it give an excuse not to go against Tia for the scholarship. Maybe it her Get Out of Jail Free card."

"How you doin' with that white boy?" Nishell asked, changing the subject so that they wouldn't be talking about Kiki when she came back.

"How it look like I'm doin'?"

"It look like you doin' good," Nishell admitted.

"I want this boy so much," Marnyke was direct. "I don't know what I wouldn't do to keep him."

"Don't get pregnant," Nishell ordered.

Marnyke gave her a little look that Nishell couldn't figure out.

Oh my god. Would she even do that?

"Marnyke!"

They looked up. Kiki stood expectantly at the door.

"Come on!" Kiki called. "Let's catch up with the guys at the basketball court!"

"Okay, orders have been given," Marnyke joked, getting to her feet.

Nishell walked them outside and said good-bye as they tromped off toward Gabe's car. Then she headed for the bus stop that would take her downtown. But instead of skyscrapers, she decided to go and photograph the old winos at Pioneer

Square. People were always a lot more interesting than things. She could walk there from here.

She hadn't taken four steps before her cell rang. The number was unfamiliar.

"Hello?" she answered.

"Hello, Nishell. It's your grandmother. Are you at work? If you're not at work, I'm coming to pick you up."

Nishell bristled. She didn't like being ordered around, and she especially didn't like being ordered around by someone she barely knew, even if that someone was a blood relative. She had four words to say to her grandmother.

"Like hell you are!"

Her grandmother didn't seem at all fazed by Nishell's strong reaction.

"You've got a backbone, Nishell Saunders. I like that."

"I don't like no one to order me around," Nishell declared.

"Then I apologize, and I'll ask another way. If you're available for a few hours this afternoon, I'd like to pick you up," her grandmother offered. "I'm sure you'll find it interesting."

"Does my mom know?" Nishell asked. She had to raise her voice over the engine noise of a passing garbage truck.

She probably in her Beemer, and I'm standing by a garbage truck. Story of our lives.

"No," Carla admitted. "But if you'd like me to e-mail her, I can do that now."

"Why you wanna see me again?" Nishell demanded.

Carla's response was immediate. "I'd like to get to know you better."

That's when Nishell got a brilliant idea. Her grandmother wanted to get to know her? Then she really needed to get to know her. See what her life was really like. Who her friends really were.

"Okay, I'm in. But I want to bring a friend."

Her grandmother said that was fine and asked her where she ought to pick her up.

"How about in front of Northeast Towers? You know where that is. Say, in an hour."

They made the date. Nishell clicked off. Then she called Jackson. He answered immediately.

"Hey, Boo, you're cuttin' into my studying."

"Funny," she responded. "Whatchu doin' now?"

"Besides waitin' for you to call? Nothing."

"Good," Nishell pronounced. "Can you meet me in front of Northeast Towers in forty-five minutes. Don't be late. And dress as thug as you can."

Nishell laughed as she saw Jackson strutting up Twenty-Third Street. She'd asked him to dress thug to shock her grandmother. He'd gone all out.

He wore a black leather cap turned sideways, a too-big black undershirt, baggy jeans that rode very low with visible red boxers underneath, and black Timberlands.

"How I look?" he said as he approached.

"Like you'd scare off any grandma I know," Nishell told him.

"As if we're meetin' your granny," Jackson joked.

"We are."

"You're kiddin' me."

Nishell shook her head. "Nope. Straight dope. She wanted to see me again. I asked if I could bring a friend. You the friend. Let's see if you scare her off."

Jackson laughed over the traffic noise. "You funnin' with her, I see. Want me to tell her I'm in the Bloods?"

Nishell raised her eyebrows. "Jackson. She won't even let you get in the car."

Ten minutes later, when her grandmother's white Beemer pulled over to the curb, Nishell got gobsmacked. Not only did her grandma allow Jackson in the car, but she greeted him warmly and insisted he sit in the front seat.

"I'm Carla Saunders," she greeted him. "Please call me Carla. Nishell does. I must say, you are an interesting young man!"

For once, Jackson had nothing to say. Neither did Nishell.

"So, where to?" Carla asked.

"Where to, what?" Nishell responded.

"You want me to see your life?" Carla asked. "Show me everything."

For the next ninety minutes, that was exactly what Nishell and Jackson did. They took Nishell's grandmother on a tour of their hood. They had her drive around Northeast Towers, up and down Twenty-Third Street, and then past the messed-up elementary and middle schools. Next stop was South Central High School. They pointed out the streets where the crack dealers did their thing and where the crack whores did theirs. They showed her the liquor stores and the auto chop shops, the after-hours clubs and the abandoned buildings, the all-night mini-marts and the all-day crowd of laborers outside the hardware store.

She wants to see it? I'm gonna show her all of it.

"Make a right here, onto Tenth Street," Nishell told her after they'd followed King Memorial Drive north for a half-mile.

"Nishell ..." Jackson cautioned. He clearly knew what was on the block.

"Nope. She wants to see everything," Nishell said grimly. "Halfway down on the left. Pull over here. Stop."

Carla pulled the BMW to the right-hand curb. They were parked directly across from a low-slung gray building badly in need of a coat of paint. Poorly dressed people streamed in and out of an open door.

"What's this?" Carla asked curiously.

"Where my mom and I lived when I was little," Nishell said flatly. "The Tenth Street Shelter. She works there still, you know. Go in and say hi if you want."

Carla kept her voice even. "Not today."

"Suit yourself," was Nishell's only comment.

"Umm, I need to get back to my studyin'," Jackson quipped.

Nishell smiled at him. "Okay. You had enough? My grand—Carla will drop you off at your place. Right, Carla?"

"Sounds fine. Which way?" Carla started the Beemer again.

Jackson lived only a few blocks from the shelter, in a walkup apartment above a mini-mart. When they reached his front stoop, Carla thanked him for coming along. So did Nishell.

"I'll text you," Jackson promised.

"Study hard," Nishell cracked.

"Word," Jackson said solemnly as he got out.

"What now?" Nishell asked. She'd climbed into the front seat, marveling at the softness of the white leather.

"Anything else you want to see of my world?"

Carla shook her head. "No. But with your permission, I'd like to show you a little bit of mine."

An hour later, Nishell was on a private guided tour of Majestic Oaks, the upscale town where her grandparents lived.

Her grandmother showed her the beautiful, oak-lined streets for which the community was named. The downtown area with its neat little shops, cute boutiques, and sidewalk cafes. The parks, golf courses, and playgrounds. No crack dealers. No crack whores. Everything clean, and everything safe.

After the tour, Carla didn't take her home. Instead, at Nishell's request, Carla drove past the house where Sierra had grown up. It was a two-story, four-bedroom dwelling surrounded by a white picket fence, with a basketball hoop on the front driveway. Nishell had never seen it before in person, though of course she'd looked it up on Google Earth.

"Wow," she breathed. "My mom grew up here."

"She did. Now I want you to see the school she attended."

It was a ten minute drive to Cranford Academy. This was another place Nishell had never seen in person. It was as big and attractive as a college campus, with a formal gate, ivy covered buildings, a huge library, and a field house. The school was laid out around an immense pond at the center of the campus.

"I'm on the board here," Carla declared. "Your grandfather and I still give them a lot of money, even though your mother never finished." She pulled the Beemer into a parking lot near the administration building. "Let's walk a little."

They got out. Nishell thought that they'd stroll around the pond. Instead, her grandmother, who had the step and energy of a woman half her age, led her past the library to a building so new there was still brown paper on the inside of the windows.

As they neared it, Nishell could read the brass plaque by the front door.

The Carla and David Saunders
Center for Fine Arts and Photography

Nishell's heart pounded in her chest. "You paid for this?"

Her grandmother smiled. "It's the finest secondary school facility of its type in the world. I daresay there are major universities that would be thrilled to have it. You enjoy photography. I thought you'd want to see it."

If I could get just one day in there. Just one—

"You could go to school here, you know," Carla said off-handedly.

"Excuse me?"

Her grandmother turned to her. "I said, you could go to school here. I could arrange it easily. You could even live with us, if you decided you didn't want to be in that small house."

Nishell stood mute, shocked at her grandmother's offer.

How much is tuition for a place like this? Forty thousand dollars a year? Fifty?

Her grandmother put her hands on Nishell's shoulders. "Let's face it, grand-daughter. You need to think about your future. You're not going to have much of one living where you are, with your mother and brother, and attending that atrocity of a high school. What I'm offering can change your life. What do you think?"

"I think …," Nishell said. "I think …"

What do I think? I have no idea.

She looked her grandmother in the eye. "I think I need to go home and do some thinking."

CHAPTER

9

Friday night was hangout night at Mio's; the night he sold slices and drinks for a buck each. It was too good a deal to resist. When Nishell got there after stopping home to change into sandals, white shorts, and a black tank top that got unwanted comments on Twenty-Third Street, she found Jackson waiting for her outside.

"You gramma has a nice ride," he joked as he embraced her.

"She got a nice school too," Nishell lamented. She'd called Jackson and told him about the rest of her afternoon.

"I just don't know what to do. And my mom's working late again. I can't talk to her till tomorrow."

"Well, check in with your homegirls," Jackson counseled.

"I will. But what do you think?"

Jackson smiled with his eyes. "Why you askin' me? I can't even get me a D on my report card."

"Because you don't try," Nishell retorted. "I mean it, Jackson. What should I do?"

"I got some thoughts, but talk to everyone first. Then you and me can talk it out."

Nishell hugged him again. This was a whole new Jackson. What she didn't know was whether it was because he was hoping she'd start hittin' it with him or whether he was changing for the better. She worried if she kept up the sex strike for too long, he'd get all hostile again. "Okay," she said.

—

They went inside and ordered three slices and two big Cokes—real for Jackson, diet for Nishell. After Mio served them up, Nishell started making the rounds. The place was packed. There were plenty of people to talk with. Jackson had been right. Everyone had an opinion.

Sherise told her that if she went to Cranford Academy, she'd be putting her social life on the line. "You just fixed things with Jackson. You think if you go to that school, he gonna take the bus out there to see you?"

"I hadn't thought of that," Nishell admitted, looking over at Jackson. He was hanging out with Carlos, laughing at some joke.

I'd miss him so much.

"Think about it now," Sherise advised.

"I could live here with my mom and drive out there."

"In what car?" Sherise asked pointedly. "Your grams gonna pay your tuition and buy you a Beemer too?"

"I don't know."

"No kidding." Sherise peeled off to go hang out with her boyfriend, Carlos Howard.

Nishell's mouth was dry from stress. She took a swallow of her diet Coke. It didn't help.

She looked around. The closest kids to her were Sean and Lattrell Chance. Lattrell had always struck her as something of a jerk, but Sean was rock steady.

Maybe I should get a guy's point of view. It can't hurt.

She approached them. "You heard about what's goin' on with me and my family?"

Lattrell nodded. "Everybody know."

"I'm wondering what you think I should do," Nishell asked.

Sean and Lattrell looked at each other.

"You wanna tell her or should I?" Lattrell asked.

"I'll tell her." Sean shifted his weight. "We was just talkin' about you. We think you gotta be careful, for different reasons. Lattrell don't trust white folks much."

"That be an understatement," Lattrell chimed in.

"And your grandma, well, she sure ain't black folks," Sean went on. "Me? I jus' don't think you're gonna like goin' to a Richie-Rich school. Those kids and you, whatchu got in common?"

"There are black kids there." Nishell had looked it up. The school was about ten percent African American.

"Yeah right," Lattrell hooted. "Black kids whose daddies run banks."

"All we're sayin' is, at least here, you be with your peeps." He looked at Lattrell. "Did I get it right?"

"Right as rain, bro'," Lattrell told him, then looked at Nishell. "I got one more thing to say. Sean be Jackson's cousin. I be his homeboy. Whatever you do? You be good to him."

Nishell thanked them and moved off. This was such a hard decision. Everything that Sherise, Lattrell, and Sean had said was true, but they weren't into photography like she was. Graduating from a school like Cranford, maybe she could become a professional.

She sighed and managed a thin little smile as Kiki and Marnyke stepped through the crowded pizzeria toward her. She thought for the hundredth time that it made no sense that these two were besties. Marnyke was all about looking hot. Kiki was all about being sporty. Somehow, they'd found common ground.

I wonder what they think.

She got an earful.

Kiki said that if Nishell went to Cranford, it was incredibly disloyal to Sierra. "Whatchu think your mother raise you for? To turn your back on her when your grandma start handin' out the chip?"

Marnyke didn't see it the same way. "You need to take care of yourself first, Nishell," she declared. "Don't worry so much 'bout your mom, or your bro, or Jackson, or the yearbook club, or nothin'. You do what best for Nishell. Nobody knows what that is better than you. If the best thing for you is to go to that school and live with your grams? Go to that school and live with your grams!"

Kiki and Marnyke both hugged her. "You our friend no matter what you decide," Kiki told her, then turned to Marnyke. "You wrong," she told her friend.

"No, you wrong!" Marnyke retorted.

That "No, you wrong!" went back and forth five or six times until they were both laughing. Then Marnyke turned back to Nishell.

"You a role model," Marnyke said. "I could never cut off Gabe like you cuttin' off Jackson. You got balls, girl."

Huh? Interesting that Marnyke had mentioned Gabe. Nishell wondered how much of what Marnyke had said to her was influenced by her relationship with the rich white boy from Majestic Oaks.

Nishell thought she'd heard enough. She looked around Mio's for Jackson, thinking that the two of them could take a walk and talk. Instead of spotting him, she saw someone unexpected step into the pizzeria.

Tia Ramirez.

Huh? Tia almost never came out on Friday nights. Tonight she was wearing black jeans and a sleeveless black blouse.

With her glasses perched atop her head, she looked very cute.

Nishell knew how smart Tia was. How driven. Suddenly, she wanted to hear what Tia thought. She cut through the crowd toward her.

"Hey," she said to Tia, ignoring dirty looks from Sherise and Kiki. "Can I buy you a slice?"

Tia smiled gratefully. "That would be great. I know there's a bunch of people here who'd just as soon I'd stay home."

"Why'd you come, then?" Nishell asked, as they moved toward the counter.

Tia learned toward Nishell and whispered. "I wanted to give Kiki something to think about."

Nishell grinned. "I think you just succeeded."

Nishell paid for a slice and a drink for Tia, and a refill of her own diet Coke. Then the two of them found the quietest table they could. Nishell laid out the whole situation with her grandmother.

"Hold on, Nishell. You're saying that your grandmother is willing to help you get into one of the top prep schools in the country, a school that has a brand new building for the photography program—and you love photography!—and you're thinking about not taking her up on it? Have you lost your mind?"

"It's complicated!" Nishell protested.

"Maybe for you! Not for me! I'd do anything to go to a better school, even if the devil was paying for it. Is your grandmother the devil?"

"Depends on who you ask," Nishell told her. "To my mom, maybe yes."

"But to you, no. Your grandmother wants to send you to a great school; she got you that great camera. Oh, by the way, I should tell you I was the one who told her about that."

Nishell sputtered soda all over the table. "You *what?*"

"When I heard your camera ended up in the river, I called her," Tia declared, as Nishell blotted at her mess with some napkins. "It wasn't hard to track her down. You needed help. I thought she could help you. I was right. Maybe I got her thinking about all this other stuff too."

"I can't believe ..." Nishell's voice trailed off. She couldn't believe that Tia was the one who had called Carla. She'd thought of everyone but Tia.

"You can't believe that I'd do that? Then you don't know me very well." Tia reached out and took Nishell's hand. "Nishell, I haven't been in America long. I'm not even a citizen of this country. Not yet. But I will tell you this. If you want something in this life, you can't wait for life to give it to you. You have to take it."

—

"Hey, Nishell. Hey, Tia."

Nishell looked up. Jackson was there.

"You 'bout ready?" Jackson asked. "I can't stay out too late. I gotta go study."

Nishell laughed. So did Tia. This whole thing Jackson had been doing these last few days about having to study was hilarious. If only there was some truth to it.

"I'm ready," Nishell told him, then turned back to Tia. "Thanks. You gave me a lot to think about."

"Do what I'd do," Tia advised.

After making the rounds and saying good-bye to their friends, Nishell and Jackson decided to head over to the Northeast Towers basketball court. Maybe there'd be a pickup game that they could watch while they talked.

For the first few minutes, they walked in silence, though Twenty-Third Street on a Friday night was hardly quiet. Passing cars with big speakers boomed hip-hop and dancehall reggae, while the sidewalks were crowded with folks of all ages enjoying the relatively cooler evening temperatures. Most people in the hood didn't have air conditioning, and it was nicer outside than inside apartments that had been baking all day in the sun.

Nishell's head hurt from all the thinking. She knew what would feel a lot better: to be someplace private with Jackson, wearing practically nothing, wrapped in each other's arms.

It was so tempting.

"Your mom home?" Nishell asked, as they neared the Northeast Towers complex.

"Nope. She won't be back till really late. How come?" Jackson asked.

"You know."

Jackson laughed. "You lookin' to take your mind off things?"

"Something like that." They turned into the complex and headed for the lit basketball court.

"Why not hold out?" Jackson suggested. "You can always break your rule another time."

Nishell took his arm. "You don't want to, if I want to?"

Jackson matched her stride for stride. "I don't want you to change your mind 'cause you stressed out. You'll be sorry afterwards."

"So what should I do?"

"About your grandmother? About the school thing? Or about hittin' it with me?"

"The first two. For now." Nishell stopped walking. They were under the sycamore trees inside the entrance to Northeast Towers, though still a hundred yards from the basketball court.

"Okay, Boo, let me break it down for you," Jackson said. "I met your grams.

She seem okay. I mean, she didn't call the cops when she saw how I dressed. But if you want to know the truth, I don't trust her. I don't trust her at all. How 'bout you?"

"I don't know," Nishell said softly. "I still don't know. And I don't know how to decide, either." She looked up at Jackson. "Can you just hold me?"

Jackson nodded. They were standing on a public walkway, but she still slid into his arms. It felt good too. Solid. Safe.

But she wasn't any closer to figuring out the right thing to do.

Nishell? Get up! Wake up if you're not awake! Come look at this video!"

Nishell was in bed on Saturday morning—she was due at the day-care at eleven—when her mother knocked on her bedroom door. She'd slept poorly, still confused over what to do about her grandmother's offer. It wasn't hard for her mother to awaken her.

"Okay, okay. I'll be right out!"

"It's Ka'lon at camp. It's fantastic!" her mother chortled.

"Okay, I'm coming!"

She pulled on an orange terrycloth bathrobe and rubbed her weary eyes. Her mom was right outside her bedroom door when she opened it, dressed in a robe of her own.

"Coffee first?" Nishell muttered.

Her mom grinned and thrust her cell at Nishell. "Nope! When you see it, you'll understand why."

Nishell pressed play. The longish video on the Fresh Air Camp website showed kids swimming, riding horses, and playing baseball.

"Where's Ka'lon?"

"Here he comes," Sierra said. "Right ... now!"

The camera zoomed in a group of kids her brother's age. Nishell picked out Ka'lon at the center of the group. They were roasting marshmallows over an open fire. Suddenly, Ka'lon held up a hand-lettered sign to the camera. The sign read, in block capital letters:

HI MOM! HI NISHELL!

Aww.

Nishell agreed that was worth being awakened for.

"Okay. Coffee's ready," her mom told her. "Then I think we need to have a talk."

"You know?" Nishell asked.

Her mom nodded and refastened the scrunchie that held back her hair in a ponytail. "My mother e-mailed me. She's getting good at that. She said she offered to send you to Cranford, and for you to live with the two of them."

"What do you think?"

Her mother pointed to the kitchen. "You wanted coffee. Go."

Nishell followed her mom to the kitchen and poured herself a steaming mug. Then the two of them moved to the living room to talk.

"Here's the e-mail." Sierra offered Nishell a folded piece of paper. "Tell me if she left anything out."

Nishell sipped her coffee as she read it through. It covered everything, even the tour of the hood that Carla had taken with Nishell and Jackson.

"It's fair," Nishell reported.

"What do you think?"

"I don't know. Everybody's givin' me different advice."

"I didn't ask what everyone was thinking, I asked what you were thinking," Sierra told her.

"I'm thinking I'm the same age now that you were then, when she and my grandfather threw you out of the house."

Nishell swung her body around to face her mother. "I'm thinkin' that for me to decide what to do now, I need to know what happened back then. Not the nice version of what happened. What really happened. How does a mother kick out her own daughter?"

Sierra winced. "You don't really want to know."

Nishell nodded. "No. I don't want to know. I *have* to know."

"Okay." Sierra looked around, as if for a cigarette. She used to smoke, but had quit several years ago. "Man, I could use a Marlboro."

"Mom? Talk."

Her mother stood, as if it was too difficult to tell this story sitting down. Then she crossed the room and gazed out the window to the street. "When I was about your age, there was this guy from the city," she told Nishell. "Wally. I've told

—

you about him. He's the one who got me pregnant. Then he took off. Even when I was pregnant with you, I knew you'd have no father."

Nishell tapped an impatient finger on her coffee mug. "Yeah. I know all that."

"But you don't know this." Sierra turned back toward Nishell. "My parents wanted me to abort you. When I said I wasn't ready to make that decision, they tried to bribe me. They offered me anything I wanted. A trip to Europe. A Porsche. A new stereo system—they had stereo systems in those days. A great graduation party. Daily sessions with a shrink. Whatever I wanted, if I would just please, please, end my pregnancy before I ruined my life!"

Nishell was speechless. She knew nothing about this part of the story. It was so intense. The baby that Carla and Dave wanted aborted had turned out to be her.

"The more they offered, the more stubborn I got," Sierra told her baldly. "No one can buy me off. No one."

"So then, they kicked you out when you said you wouldn't do it?" Nishell asked.

"They said that if I wanted to ruin my life, they were not going to be a part of it. They took my car keys, cancelled my enrollment at school, and changed the locks on their doors," Sierra recalled bitterly. "I couldn't come home even if I wanted to."

Nishell studied the surface of her coffee, as if the secret to how parents could be so angry at their own child could somehow be found in the warm, brown liquid.

What about a mother's love? God, Carla is cold. Mom's not like her at all. She would support me no matter what.

"I'm sorry," Nishell said quietly. "And thankful. If you didn't do what you decided to do, there'd be no me."

Sierra stepped across the living room, sat by Nishell, and hugged her. "I love you so much, Nishell. I've never been sorry for what I decided. Not a single day. I love you so much that I want you to know that whatever you decide, I'll love you just as much."

"Your parents never contacted you again?" Nishell asked.

Sierra shook her head. "They did. But I was so hurt—am so hurt—I didn't want to see them. I still don't. It'll mess me up."

"Maybe that can change."

"Maybe."

Then, like a flash of wisdom from God in heaven, Nishell knew the right thing to do. For herself. For her grandparents. For her mom and her brother.

"I'd like to help with that," Nishell told her. "I think I can do that better if I'm here. Yeah, it's tempting, what your mom is offering. But it ain't tempting enough."

She put her arms out to her mother. They embraced. This one went on for a long, long time.

There was a little outdoor café down by the river—more like a few plastic tables and chairs, with a shack that sold drinks and snacks. When Jackson had asked Nishell to meet when she came off work, Nishell had suggested the café.

She'd called her grandmother right after her conversation with Sierra, but Carla hadn't picked up. Nishell had left a voicemail with her decision, inviting Carla to call her back. So far, Carla hadn't. Nishell wasn't sure that she would.

Then she'd called Jackson. He was happy to hear the news and said he was studying. It made Nishell laugh all over again.

Now she was alone at one of the tables. She'd brought her camera. She was zooming in on an extremely fat squirrel when Jackson came running over, holding a white envelope. He wore basketball shorts and a red T-shirt.

"Hey, hey, here comes the scholar," he announced.

"Funny," she told him, taking one last shot of the tubby squirrel. He'd crawled head-first into a potato chip bag on the ground, so only his bushy tail showed.

"No, I'm straight up," Jackson said.

"It's too bad you flunked all those classes," Nishell told him. "My mom texted me before; she's got another date with the landscape dude tonight. My apartment be empty till midnight."

"Oh really?" Jackson asked. He pushed the unmarked envelope across the table toward Nishell, then sat. "Check it out."

"What is it?"

"Just open it," Jackson said with a grin.

Nishell did. She took out a single sheet of paper. As she read what was written on the paper, her jaw went slack. It was a grade report from the state online high school program for 11th grade algebra home study. Jackson was in summer school!

Jackson had earned a B+.

"I told you I was studying," he declared.

"Jackson! Omigod! You got a B-plus!" Nishell threw her arms around him and whooped so loudly that people passing by stared at them. "B-plus! B-plus!"

"Of course I can do it," Jackson said with dignity. "And I will fix all my failing grades. I'm lazy, not stupid. So I got just one question."

The minute she saw the good grade on the printout, Nishell knew what was coming. She also knew that Jackson had never looked finer than he did right now. She wanted him. She wanted him desperately. Best of all, he'd passed the test.

"We good to go?" he asked.

She smiled coyly. "I don't know. I like what I see on that exam. But can you keep it up?"

He smiled back. "I'm highly motivated. A-squared plus B-squared equals C-squared."

"Equals me squared," Nishell murmured back. "That means you have to kiss me again."

"What if you don't really want to?" Jackson asked.

Nishell smiled. "Well then, I'd say you ought to tempt me."